THE SWAN BOAT RIDE

Written by
FRANCES DRISCOLL

Illustrated by
ANNIE KANE O'CONNOR

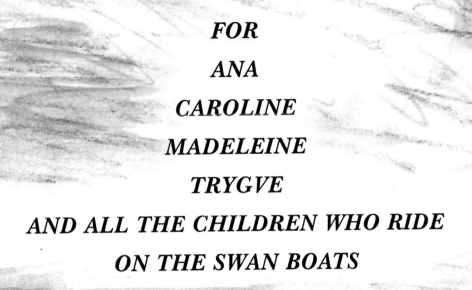

FOR
ANA
CAROLINE
MADELEINE
TRYGVE
AND ALL THE CHILDREN WHO RIDE
ON THE SWAN BOATS

"Il faut regarder toute la vie avec des yeux d'enfant."

— HENRI MATISSE

All your life, you must see with a child's eyes.

When I woke up, I knew it was going to be a special day!

Grandma was taking my two sisters and me to the Boston Public Garden so we could ride on the Swan Boats. Grandma said that people come from all over the world to ride on the Swan Boats.

"Hurry up!" I called to my sisters as I ran out the front door. "Don't forget to put your lunch in your backpack!" We walked down the street with Grandma to the T station.

Some people were already there waiting for the train. One lady was talking on her cell phone and a man was writing in a small notebook, but they both looked up when we heard the train.

"Oh! Here comes the train!" I could see it coming along the tracks. When it stopped and the doors opened, we hopped on the train.

There were lots of people on the train with us so we had to hold on tightly.

There was a man wearing a necktie, a lady holding a baby, and some big boys who were laughing.

I thought, "Wow! Are all these people going to ride on the Swan Boats, too?"

When the train reached Arlington Street we stepped off and went up the escalator to the street. My sister turned and asked, "Grandma, are the Swan Boats as big as the train…with lots of people? Are the swans real?"

"You will see," said Grandma. I loved riding up the escalator.

We crossed the street and entered the Public Garden. As we walked toward the pond, we stopped to see the pretty tulips; all shades of pink, red, yellow, purple, and lavender. "Hmm… the flowers smell like perfume," said my sister happily as she knelt down to smell them. "Look, Grandma," I said, "Those tall trees have branches that droop all the way down to the water!" "Yes, those trees are called weeping willow trees," Grandma replied.

"Oh, look over there," I pointed, "there are two Swan Boats in the water; TWO beautiful swans are following the boats. Oh! Those swans are REAL!"

One Swan Boat was going under the bridge. That looked like so much fun. My youngest sister said, "Look! All the people on the boat are smiling at us! Where is the boat going?
Is it coming back?" "You will see!" said Grandma

We stood on the platform as the Swan Boat pulled up in front of us. Stepping onto the boat, I slid to the edge of the seat so that I could see everything in the water. My two sisters sat next to me, then Grandma. The man who peddles the boat like a bicycle was sitting at the back. Slowly, the boat began sliding away from the dock, moving smoothly like a swan swimming around the pond.

Some ducks swam right
near our boat, turning
their heads to look at us.
"Quack! Quack!" they said.
"Quack! Quack!"
we said back.
"Hello to you, too!"

The two beautiful swans swam close to our boat. "I read in the newspaper that their names are Romeo and Juliet," said Grandma. I studied their long, white necks and their feathers. "They look so soft and silky," I said. "I wish I could pet them!"

"Me, too! Me, too!" my sisters said. The water around them was sparkling in the sunshine. Romeo stared at us seriously, staying as still as a statue.

Juliet was friendly and swam alongside our Swan Boat. As she swam, Juliet turned her head to us. I smiled at her. And, do you know what happened?

JULIET SMILED BACK AT ME!

Now, it was our turn to go under the bridge. People up on the bridge waved and smiled at us. "Don't worry!" my youngest sister yelled. "We'll be back! Right, Grandma?" We all waved back and smiled, too. As our Swan Boat moved along, we saw the big nest on the grass where Juliet sits on her eggs.

Then, our boat began to turn and I could see many, many ducks swimming. I counted them out loud, "One, two, three, four…" I went all the way up to thirty-two! "Quack! Quack!" said the ducks. "Quack! Quack!" we said back.

Too soon our Swan Boat ride was over. "We'll come back to see you!" I called as I turned and waved good-bye to Romeo and Juliet.

Afterward, we found a shady spot on the grass near the edge of the water to spread our blanket for our picnic. I opened my lunch and found my favorite: a peanut butter and jelly sandwich, a bag of baby carrots and cucumber slices, and a container of green grapes. Everything tasted so delicious!

When we finished our lunch, Grandma said it was time to go home. My two sisters and I walked with Grandma back through the Public Garden towards the street.

Just before we crossed the street, my youngest sister said, "That was a fun day, Grandma. Can we come back again soon?" Grandma smiled, "Yes, we will come back". "I want to see Juliet smile again!" I said. "Me, too! Me, too!" my sisters yelled.

We all smiled, crossed the street, and walked into the T station.

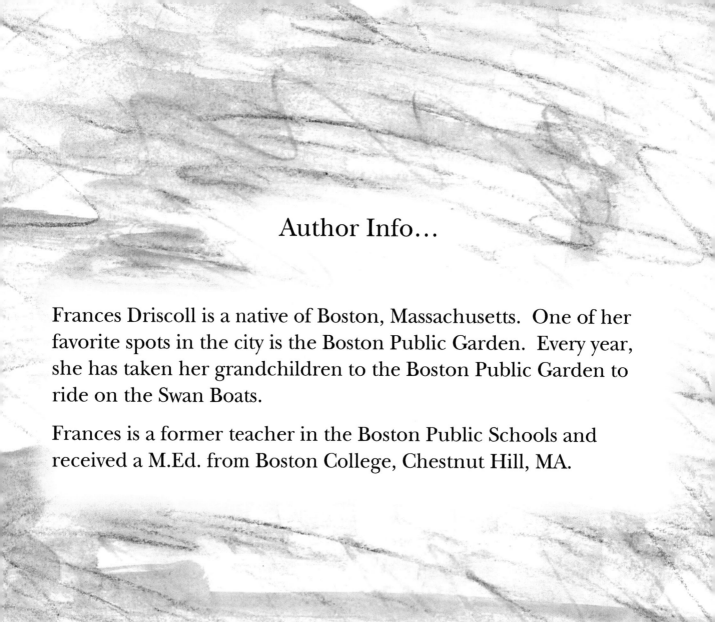

Author Info…

Frances Driscoll is a native of Boston, Massachusetts. One of her favorite spots in the city is the Boston Public Garden. Every year, she has taken her grandchildren to the Boston Public Garden to ride on the Swan Boats.

Frances is a former teacher in the Boston Public Schools and received a M.Ed. from Boston College, Chestnut Hill, MA.

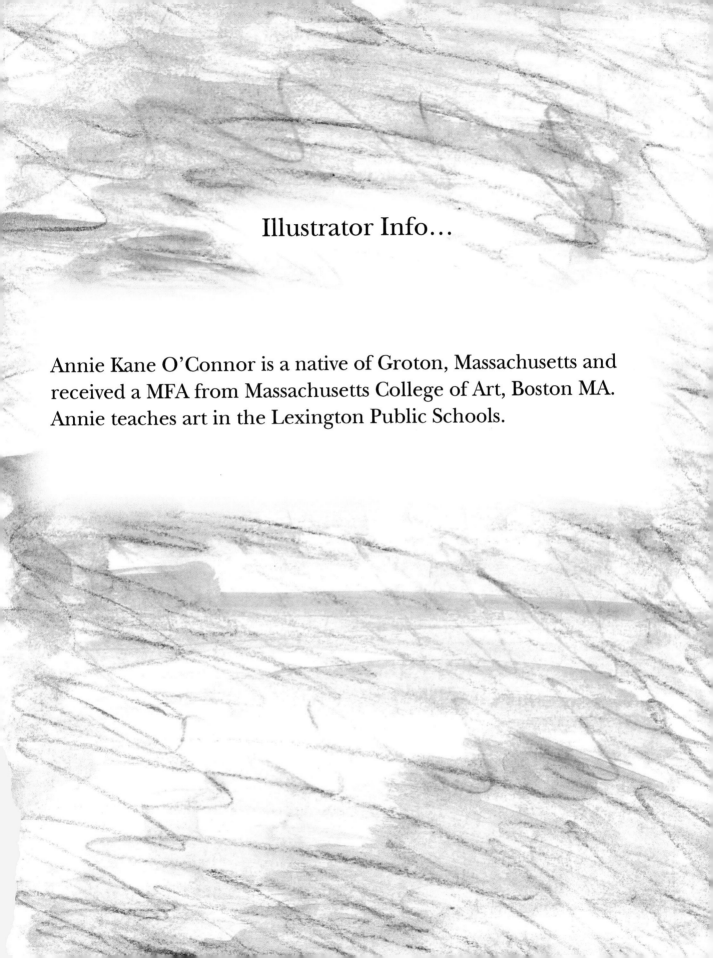

Illustrator Info…

Annie Kane O'Connor is a native of Groton, Massachusetts and received a MFA from Massachusetts College of Art, Boston MA. Annie teaches art in the Lexington Public Schools.

Made in the USA
Charleston, SC
07 April 2014